Different

PRAISE FOR *STORYSHARES*

"One of the brightest innovators and game-changers in the education industry."
– Forbes

"Your success in applying research-validated practices to promote literacy serves as a valuable model for other organizations seeking to create evidence-based literacy programs."

- Library of Congress

"We need powerful social and educational innovation, and Storyshares is breaking new ground. The organization addresses critical problems facing our students and teachers. I am excited about the strategies it brings to the collective work of making sure every student has an equal chance in life."
– Teach For America

"Around the world, this is one of the up-and-coming trailblazers changing the landscape of literacy and education."
- International Literacy Association

"It's the perfect idea. There's really nothing like this. I mean wow, this will be a wonderful experience for young people."   - Andrea Davis Pinkney, Executive Director, Scholastic

"Reading for meaning opens opportunities for a lifetime of learning. Providing emerging readers with engaging texts that are designed to offer both challenges and support for each individual will improve their lives for years to come. Storyshares is a wonderful start."
- David Rose, Co-founder of CAST & UDL

Different

Jennie Ford

STORYSHARES

Story Share, Inc.
New York. Boston. Philadelphia

Storyshares
Story Share, Inc.
24 N. Bryn Mawr Avenue #340
Bryn Mawr, PA 19010-3304
www.storyshares.org

Inspiring reading with a new kind of book.

Interest Level: High School
Grade Level Equivalent: 2.8

9781973491309

Book design by Storyshares

Printed in the United States of America

Storyshares Presents

1

If I'm going to sing like someone else, then I don't need to sing at all.

\- Billie Holiday

When I was younger, the water stain on my ceiling reminded me of a duck.

I now laid on my bed and stared at the yellow splotch directly above me and saw nothing but the ugliness of our old house. I wished I still had those younger eyes that could find things interesting, eyes that saw things beyond the cold, hard truth.

"Caleb?" Mom knocked and opened the door. "Caleb, your Dad's mowing. You could help, you know."

"He didn't ask me to help," I said.

She stood and looked at me. She seemed tired, as usual. She took a deep breath and I knew what was coming next. "Please get up and get out of your room." She took another deep breath. "You worry me. Is something bothering you?"

"No, Mom, I'm just tired."

"You're always tired. Get up...go outside...get some fresh air," she said.

"I'm fine, Mom. Please leave me alone."

"Where are your friends? Why don't you hang out anymore?" she asked. "I haven't seen Wyatt in forever, or what's his name...the little scrawny one?" She looked to the ceiling, thinking. "Jonathan, isn't that his name?"

"I guess, Mom."

"You guys used to have so much fun playing your guitars and listening to music. You haven't picked your guitar up in ages." She walked to the corner where my guitar was propped and ran her fingers across it. "It's dusty. That's a shame. You used to love this guitar. You saved and saved your money for it. I think that may have been the happiest I've ever seen you, when you brought this home."

She took the tail of her shirt and dusted it. She smiled the smile you make when thinking of a good memory. I felt bad now that I was being a big brat to her.

"I'm okay. I promise," I said.

"You can talk to me, you know," she said quietly, staring me in the eyes.

"I'm okay, Mom. You're making a big deal out of nothing."

"Am I?" she asked.

"Yes," I told her.

"Supper will be ready soon. I want you to eat at the table, okay?"

"Sure," I said. I took another hard look at the yellowed splotch on my ceiling and tried to see a duck.

I couldn't.

I forced myself off the bed and sat on its edge. I cleared my head and looked around. I got up and walked to my computer. It too was covered in the dust of an old house. I ran my fingers over it. This used to be my baby. I ordered it piece by piece. When I finally got the last one, me and my buddies spent a whole day building it. It was perfection. We celebrated with high fives and pizza and played rounds of Counter Strike half the night!

How long ago was that? I thought about it. Three months ago. It seemed like forever.

I could hear my mom and dad talking on the front porch while Dad brushed grass from his pantlegs.

"Don't worry honey," Dad said. "It's probably just girl problems."

2

I walked the halls of high school with my head down. I wore the same t-shirt from yesterday and the same worn jeans. I no longer heard the voices screaming down the hall, "Caleb! My man! Caleb, what's up! Caleb!" Instead I walked in silence.

My friends, they weren't mean to me. My friends were ghosts. They had known me since preschool. They told secrets to me. We hung out. We were tight.

Not anymore. Not since I told my very best friend in the entire world that I was confused. My best friend in the entire world was Kayla. We'd grown up together in a state subsidized daycare. We'd played in the after school program in elementary school. Kayla was like a sister to me.

Until I told her I was confused. That's all.

We used to talk for hours on the phone, on Skype. We would talk about life. We talked about getting a place when we graduated. We talked about how her parents drank too much and about how my parents worked too much. We talked about everything.

But I should have never told her that I thought I was gay.

Now she sat behind me in web design class.

"Ew, your book bag is leaning on mine. Move it," Kayla said. I looked at her and searched her face for anything recognizable as my friend but I couldn't find it. I moved my bag away from hers, and saw Wyatt and Chris and little Jonathan shake their heads slowly in disgust. I lowered my head and thought of nothing but blackness. The bell rang and forced me to rise and make my way to the next class.

3

"Caleb? Can I come in?" It was Mom. She had on her scrubs from work. When did I ever see her without those damned scrubs?

"Yes, Mom."

"Caleb, I'm making you a doctor's appointment."

"Why Mom?"

"Because, I'm worried about you...that's why."

"Mom, I'm fine. Jesus, why do you want to always make me feel bad?"

Mom lowered her head."I don't. I mean, I don't mean to."

I was the youngest of four kids. My mom had had me when she was forty. My siblings were grown with families of their own. Mom did try to stay hip. She tolerated my music and actually seemed to like it. She listened to me while I talked endlessly about a video game or a YouTube channel. She kept an open mind to all of my interests.

Why I didn't trust her with my deepest, darkest secret is something I cannot explain. Why had I trusted Kayla Jennings? I thought we were friends 'til the end! I don't know.

It shouldn't be this hard.

"I think you're depressed, Caleb," Mom said. "You're always tired and you're not eating well. You're not enjoying life anymore." She became teary.

"Don't cry, Mom, please." I hated to see her cry. If I told her the truth...if I told her what was really going on, I imagined I would see many more tears. I couldn't do that to her.

"I'm just worried about college, you know...my future," I told her. She sat on my bed and rubbed the top of my head.

"Caleb, it will be okay. I thought you had decided on Western State?"

That was something else I couldn't tell her. My grades were bad. I was flunking everything. My GPA had dropped. I wouldn't be able to get into Western.

"I don't know, Mom. Maybe," I said.

"Cheer up...please?" she pleaded.

"I will, Mom."

She wiped her eyes and tried to smile. "Dad's grilling burgers tonight," she said before closing my door.

"That sounds great," I said, and made a small smile back.

Once she was gone, I held myself. I wrapped my arms around me as hard as I could. And I cried like I was five years old.

4

Janelle Thompson sat alone in the lunch room. She had sat alone most everyday since first grade. She'd been dealt a crappy hand in this crappy society we live in.

She had coarse, red hair that grew big and untamable on her head. Her features were quite manly and her body quite thick. It was sad, no...horrible, the way she was kicked out of the group for merely being born unattractive. And I had always been one of those kicking.

I watched her a little more closely now. Now I found myself moved to tears for her. I saw her wearing the right clothes. She had the name brands that were popular. Was she wearing makeup? Yes, she was trying. She was doing all she could to stay on the perimeter and not completely disappear.

Janelle Thompson had lived like this her whole life. What did she do when she went home? Did she lie in her bed and cry? Did she work with her makeup and hair? Did she stare in the mirror and curse her genes?

I wanted to ask her. I wanted to go sit and talk to her and ask her what she does to stay sane.

Will her life get better? Will it get better when she leaves this town, this school, these people? I hoped so. I really hoped so.

I walked to where Janelle was sitting.

"Hey Janelle," I said.

"Hi Caleb," she answered, a little hesitant.

"Janelle, I just wanted to tell you that you look beautiful today."

She jumped slightly as if someone had given her a little pinch. And then, she smiled. She smiled so big.

"Th-Thank you, Caleb," she said.

"You're welcome, Janelle."

Different

5

"Son?"

I looked up from my bowl of cereal to see Dad standing tall, hands on his hips.

"I've got to take the old mower to the shop...want to ride with me? I'll buy lunch," he said.

"I'm eating."

"No, you're not. You're staring at it and I don't blame you. Doesn't look very appetizing." He smiled. "Come on, go with me."

"Sure, okay," I said.

We loaded the old mower onto his truck bed.

"Dad, watch your back," I said.

"I'm fine. I'm being careful," he said.

Dad had to have back surgery a few months ago. His spine was full of arthritis. He stayed in a lot of pain. But he never let it get him totally down. Even after the surgery, when Mom urged him to take the pain pills, he more often than not refused them.

We sailed down the highway with Dad blasting music from a classic rock station. He tapped his fingers on the steering wheel along with the beat.

"So Caleb, whatever happened to that little girl friend of yours. The cute one?" Dad asked.

"I don't know who you're talking about," I lied.

"Chloe, that's her name. The little blonde," Dad said. "You were sweet on her, I thought."

"Just friends, Dad."

"What about Kayla? Where has she been?" he asked.

"Busy, I guess," I said.

Dad shook his head in understanding. "You'll find you one, no worries. It's good to play the field."

"Maybe I don't like girls," I said.

Dad's fingers stopped drumming. He looked at me. "You're a hoot, son, a real hoot." He laughed. "Where do you want to eat lunch?"

Different

6

William Waldrop wore a dress shirt and bow tie to school every day. He had since fifth grade. He was the school nerd/activist. One rarely saw him without a clip board begging for signatures for some sort of social injustice. He petitioned for better school lunches, for town park renovations, for climate change. Most kids considered him whacky. That fact didn't seem to bother him.

He stood in the hallway between classes asking for a moment of his classmates' time. He handed out pamphlets explaining each of his causes. The pamphlets were often seen littering the floors and the waste baskets.

I wondered if anything he did mattered. Had he ever changed anything? Was it worth the taunting from his classmates? I watched him stand tall with his clipboard. He was often pushed and ran into in the busy hallway.

"Get out of my way, weirdo."

"Freak."

"You're pathetic."

"Fag."

His classmates hated him. Why? I tried to wrap my head around it! Why was he treated so horribly? He wasn't hurting anyone.

He was just... different.

I was fast learning that being different was dangerous. It shouldn't be, but somehow, it was. That thought put a chill in me. Would it get better for him? Would he find other people like him? I hoped so.

"Hey, William, what you got there?" I asked.

"Oh, Caleb, hi. I'm asking for petitions to stop big oil companies from taking and polluting the American Indian lands. Here, take this pamphlet and educate yourself," he said.

"Thanks, I will," I said. "Can I sign your petition?"

"Sure, yes. Thank you!" He smiled.

I proudly signed my name beneath the signature of Janelle Thompson.

Different

7

I opened the medicine cabinet, searching for something to ease my aching head. I reached for a bottle of aspirin and my hand brushed against a prescription bottle. It was my father's and it read: Take one every 4 to 6 hours for back pain.

I picked it up and shook it. It was almost full. I stared at the bottle for a moment. I put it back in its place and grabbed the aspirin. I ran into Mom as I rushed out. I jumped.

"God, Mom, you scared me," I said.

"Are we jumpy today?" she asked.

"No, why should I be?" I said.

She gave me a funny look. "I'm just playing with you, Caleb. Lighten up, please."

"Whatever, Mom," I said and went around her.

"Caleb, will you please straighten up your room?" she called. "Your brothers and sister will be here tomorrow. Remember? Thanksgiving? Our favorite time of year?"

"Sure."

"I've got to run to the store...you want to go with me?" Mom asked. "I'll buy you a mocha latte."

"No, thanks."

"Okay, well...I'll be back shortly," she said.

I watched out the window as she backed her old VW out of the garage and to the road. I watched until she was out of sight and then I went back to the bathroom.

Maybe she forgot something and would have to come back, I thought suddenly. I ran back to the front window to make sure she was gone.

She was. I opened the medicine cabinet and grabbed the prescription bottle of pain pills and shook them out into my hand. I counted fourteen in my palm. I put the rest back. I walked to my room and hid the pills in the pocket of a jacket hanging in my closet. My hands were shaking. Dad's truck pulled into the drive. I closed my closet door.

Different

8

The first to arrive for the Thanksgiving festivities were my sister Erin and her husband Mark. They were both school teachers. I could expect the usual questions from her about my grades and my plans. I could expect the usual scolding she gave my Mom for babying me too much. Fun.

Next was my brother Christopher and his wife Diane. They drove in from Charlotte. He was some sort of business man with a large utility company. I didn't know exactly what he did. I knew he wore a suit and he made great money. He came in with ironed khakis and a nice sweater. His wife was an accountant. She was over dressed and too perfumed.

Dad was anxiously awaiting for Chris to arrive so he could check out his new sports car. I could expect questions from Christopher about how dating was going. He would inquire about my conquests of high school girls and give me a nudge and a silly grin.

Last was my brother Sam, his wife April, and their six year old son, Jack, who was named after our Grandpa. Sam still drove the Honda he'd had in college. It was old and worn. The car's blue paint was faded off the hood. Sam worked at the mill and April worked at the drug store. He wore a flannel shirt and work boots. April wore jeans and a blouse.

"Nice car you got there, Chris," Sam said.

"Thanks, I love it," Chris answered. Everyone hugged and commented on how grown up Jack was getting.

"He's smart like his Daddy," April bragged. The room grew a little quiet for a moment until Mom said, "Yes, he is, and that's wonderful."

9

Erin and Diane followed Mom into the kitchen. Dad, Chris and Mark found a football game to watch. Jack grabbed April's hand and made her go with him to Sam's old room. It now served as his toy room.

Sam found me sitting on the couch trying to act interested in the loud football game.

"You and me, downstairs. The best two out of three games of pool determines the world championship," Sam said.

"Nah," I said.

"Come on. I'll go easy on ya, I promise." He smiled.

"I guess," I said. He was impossible to resist.

The basement was dusty and hanging with cobwebs. "This place looks terrible. Don't you ever come down here?" Sam asked.

"No," I said.

"Well, it sure needs a cleaning. I'll come over one weekend when I'm off work and we'll clean it up," he said.

"Sure," I said.

He dusted off the green felt of the pool table with a large brush. "Hey, did you check out Chris' car? Wow. That must've set him back," Sam said.

"No," I said.

"I didn't either. I didn't want to see him gloat." He smiled. "I see Diane hasn't changed a bit," Sam made a snooty face and stuck his nose in the air.

"You're terrible," I said and made a small chuckle.

Sam still had a little boy face and sandy hair that was thick and wavy. "So, what's up with you? You look awful. You've lost weight," Sam said.

"Thanks," I said.

"I'll rack the first game," he said. "And after that the loser racks."

Sam beat me three straight games in less than thirty minutes. "Are you even trying?" he asked. "Three more games for the championship of the universe," Sam said.

"No thanks," I said.

"Okay, go back up there and suffer passive aggressive remarks from your sister. Me, I'll pass." Sam smiled. He held his pool stick and propped himself up on a barstool. "You okay, buddy?" he asked seriously.

"Yes," I said.

"You know, I was nine years old when you were born and let me tell you, I was pissed."

"Why?" I asked.

"Because I wasn't the baby anymore and that sucked. Being the baby has its perks, man."

"You're crazy," I said.

"Am I? I now was a big brother and I was supposed to give you someone to look up to. That's a lot on a guy." Sam shifted on the stool and thought about his next words. "When I was just a couple years older than you are now, I was in my sophomore year of college. I had gotten a full ride to UNC on academics. I was the big man on campus, loving life. Then one day, April tells me she's pregnant."

"I already know this story," I said.

"You don't know it all," he said. "You don't know what happened to me."

"What happened?" I asked.

10

"I thought my life was over. I didn't want to face Mom and Dad. I couldn't tell them. They were so proud of me getting a scholarship. They bragged on me. I thought this would kill them. I cried. I couldn't eat. I thought, how was I supposed to raise a child? I didn't even know if I wanted to spend the rest of my life with April. One of the biggest things I worried about was seeing disappointment in Mom and Dad's eyes. Honestly, I wanted to die."

"What helped?" I asked.

"I had to gather my strength and tell them," he said. "And when I did, boy, it was like a million pounds of crap suddenly lifted off my shoulders. Mom and Dad are cooler than you think, Caleb...remember that."

"I will," I said.

"I wish you were old enough to remember Grandpa Jack. He was the best. He took me fishing one day soon after Grandma died. He told me that when she died he didn't think he could go on, but he did. He said, life is tough, but it's worth every precious minute."

"He sounds cool. Sam, did Mom ask you to talk to me?" I asked.

"Yes, she did," he said.

I shook my head and made a small grin. "It's good to see you, Sam. I do miss you," I said.

"You call me if you ever need me, little bro. Okay?" Sam said.

"Sam, is there anything that I could do to make you not want to be my brother?" I asked.

Sam sat and pondered my question. He rubbed his chin and looked into space.

"Maybe if you were a serial killer," he said. "Or a white supremacist, or a child abuser, or a... I'm thinking..."

"Or gay?" I asked.

Sam stopped and looked me.

I couldn't look at him and lowered my head.

He walked to me and hugged me. "Thank God. I thought you had gotten a young lady pregnant," he joked.

I started to laugh. It was a welcome laugh. It brought tears to my eyes. He laughed, too.

It felt good.

"Sam, I don't want to be different," I said seriously.

Sam took my face in both his hands and looked me in the eyes. "Different? Caleb, you are the same person now that you were the day you were born. You are not different. And you're going to have to talk to Mom and Dad. You're going to have to get this out of you. You can't keep this in, Caleb," Sam said.

"I'm going to," I said.

"I'll be there with you if you want me to," he said.

"Thanks Sam, but I will do it myself," I said.

"A little advice, Caleb. You must remember that it didn't take you a day to figure all this out about yourself. I'm sure it's been something you have been coming to grips with for a while now. Right?"

"Yes," I said.

"Don't expect Mom and Dad to come to terms with this overnight either. It will take them awhile, but they will. And it will not change how they feel about you. How any of us do. Okay?"

"Thank you, Sam," I said.

11

I looked out my window and saw Jack throwing rocks in a puddle. I put on my jacket and joined him.

"Caleb, do you want to throw rocks with me?" he asked.

"Yes, I do," I said.

His eyes grew big with excitement. "The best rocks are over here, Caleb. See?" he said.

"These are great rocks," I said. "Good find."

"Yes!" he agreed.

We stood side by side and splashed as many rocks as we could find into the muddy water.

"Watch this!" Caleb said. He twirled his little arm around and around. He had a serious look on his face as he heaved the rock as hard as he could and made a mighty splash.

"Good one!" I cheered.

"Jack, we're getting ready to leave! Come tell everyone goodbye!" April yelled out the front door.

"Guess it's time to go in," I said.

"Caleb, will the puddle be here next time I come over?" Jack asked.

"I'm not sure, maybe it will," I said.

"Caleb, will you be here?" he asked.

I smiled and said, "Yes, I will."

Epilogue

Suicide is the 2nd leading cause of death among young people ages 10-24.

The rate of suicide attempts is 4 times greater for LGBTQIA youth and 2 times greater for questioning youth.

LGBTQIA youth who come from highly rejecting families are 8.4 times as likely to have attempted suicide as peers who reported low or no levels of family rejection.

1 out of 6 students nationwide seriously considered suicide last year.

There are resources available.

You are not alone.

It will get better.

The number for the Trevor lifeline is: 866-488-7386.

You can also chat at www.thetrevorproject.org.

The National Youth crisis hotline can be reached at crisistextline.org or text Go to 741741.

About The Author

Jennie Ford is a mother, writer, potter, and artist. Jennie was raised in Eastern North Carolina, where the rich farming landscapes provide the backdrop to many of her stories.

As a contributor to Storyshares for many years, she will continue to compose short stories for their expanding library. Now residing in Western North Carolina, Jennie is currently writing a novel for young adult readers, which she hopes to publish in the future.

About The Publisher

Story Shares is a nonprofit focused on supporting the millions of teens and adults who struggle with reading by creating a new shelf in the library specifically for them. The ever-growing collection features content that is compelling and culturally relevant for teens and adults, yet still readable at a range of lower reading levels.

Story Shares generates content by engaging deeply with writers, bringing together a community to create this new kind of book. With more intriguing and approachable stories to choose from, the teens and adults who have fallen behind are improving their skills and beginning to discover the joy of reading. For more information, visit storyshares.org.

Easy to Read. Hard to Put Down.

Made in the USA
Middletown, DE
20 January 2023

22671424R00031